Cataloguing-in-Publication data for this book is available from the Library of Congress (LC Control No. 2010909625).

Published by Posture & Breathing, LLC
PO Box 785
Oakhurst, NJ 07755
Email: postureandbreathing@gmail.com

Publisher's Note

Dedication

I would like to dedicate this book to my family. My parents, who loved me and supported my decision to become a physical therapist. My husband, without whom I would not have completed this book and who is always there to listen and offer suggestions. My children Tamar, Erez, Oren and Hadas who love me, guide me and always provide advice. My daughter Tamar, her husband Cam and their daughters Rachel and Kaila, who provided the inspiration for this book.

I would also like to extend my gratitude to all my patients, who have and continue to teach me about the depths of love, patience, courage and how to move forward without giving up.

Thank you to my teachers, co-workers, friends and family for all of the guidance that you provided me throughout my life.

Love, Yaffa Liebermann

I Stand Up Straight
Poem and Exercises
By Yaffa Liebermann, Physical Therapist

Poem co-written by Livia Beasley
Illustrated by Katie Sokolowski

1

When the sun rises,
I wake up from sleep,
and I straighten up,
from my head to my feet.

And Mommy says…
Hold your head up,
and be proud.
Stand up straight,
now, sing out loud:
"Head, shoulders,
tummy, feet,
stand up tall,
it's really neat!"

Head!
It's time to stand tall
so I lift up my head
like being pulled
up by a long thread.

And Teacher says...
Hold your head up,
and be proud.
Stand up straight,
now, sing out loud:
"Head, shoulders,
tummy, feet,
stand up tall,
it's really neat!"

Shoulders!
Hold my shoulders back.
And keep my chest out.
That gives my lungs space
to breathe in and out.

And Daddy says...
Hold your head up,
and be proud.
Stand up straight,
now, sing out loud:
"Head, shoulders,
tummy, feet,
stand up tall,
it's really neat!"

Tummy!
Tuck in my tummy
and keep my back straight.
This strengthens my body
and makes me feel great.

And Grandma says…

Hold your head up,
and be proud.
Stand up straight,
now, sing out loud:
"Head, shoulders,
tummy, feet,
stand up tall,
it's really neat!"

Feet!

I point my feet forward
and keep my ankles straight.
I don't lock my knees
and keep equal weight.

And Grandpa says...
Hold your head up,
and be proud.
Stand up straight,
now, sing out loud:
"Head, shoulders,
tummy, feet,
stand up tall,
it's really neat!"

And I say...
I look in the mirror.
"I'm standing up straight!"
I'm looking so good
and I'm feeling great!

Notes for Caregiver
Posture Checklist
Exercise Guidelines
Correct Posture (Front and Side View)
Exercises

Notes for Caregivers

Use this book as a tool to teach children correct posture in a fun and creative manner.

The body was designed to be lined up in a certain way to get the best muscle function and joint movements. When we stand up straight, we give room to the vital organs to function well. When shoulders are pulled back and the chest is up, we give our lungs room to breathe.

Feet are the body's base. Therefore, shoes are a priority when dressing a child. Shoes should fit comfortably (not too tight), be stiff around the heel, and have small, built-in arch supports.

Good posture needs to be maintained through understanding and practice. When we maintain an upright posture, it contributes to good self esteem. Encourage your child to stand in front of the mirror and practice correct posture. The caregiver should also set an example by practicing and maintaining good posture.

Posture Checklist

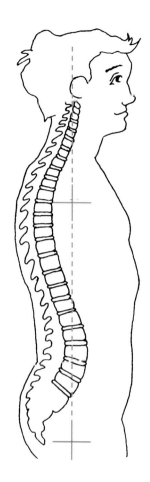

- ❑ Head up and chin tucked in above the notch between the collarbones.
- ❑ Chin is parallel to the floor.
- ❑ Tongue on the palate (like saying the letter L).
- ❑ Shoulders are leveled, pulled back but not tight.
- ❑ Upper back straight, so chest bone is up.
- ❑ Arms hang easily at the sides with the palm toward the body.
- ❑ Abdominal wall tightened.
- ❑ Lower back is slightly curved forward.
- ❑ Hips are level.
- ❑ Kneecaps face straight ahead, knees straight, 'easy' but not bent, not pushed back and not 'locked'.
- ❑ Feet are pointed straight forward while toes pointing slightly out.
- ❑ Weight is falling over the arch, equally balanced between the ball and the front of the feet.
- ❑ Weight should be equally distributed to both feet.

Exercise Guidelines

In the following pages are a few exercises that can be performed in any environment. They can be performed separately or in a series. Follow a 'no-discrimination' policy: use both sides of the body equally (right and left) and exercise opposing muscle groups (abdominal and back muscles). Maintaining equal balance will help give the body a natural cast and form good alignment. Practice breathing continuously throughout the exercises.

If the child has had any pre-existing physical conditions or experiences difficulty during these exercises, it is advisable to consult a doctor. Adjust the exercises to fit the child's abilities and needs.

Most importantly – enjoy and make it fun.

Correct Posture
(Front View)

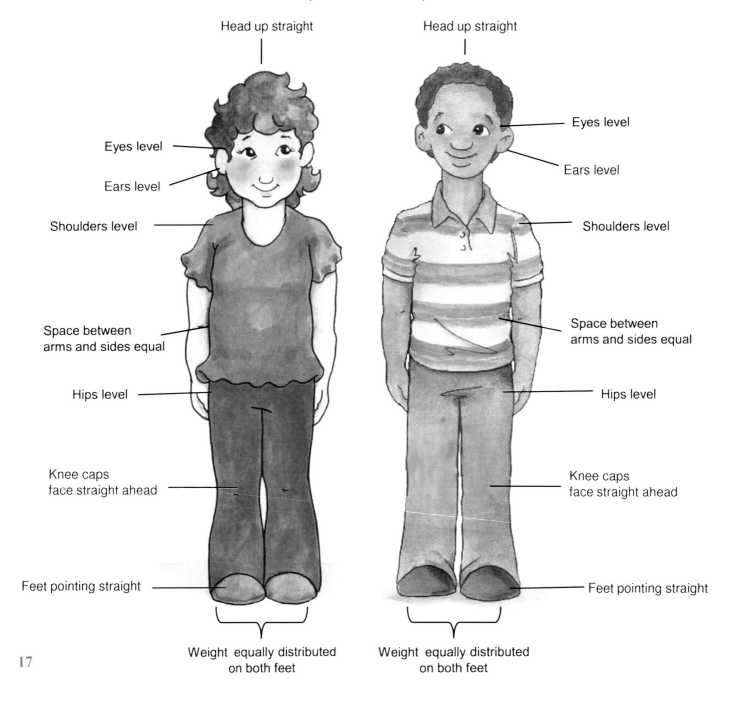

Head up straight

Head up straight

Eyes level

Eyes level

Ears level

Ears level

Shoulders level

Shoulders level

Space between arms and sides equal

Space between arms and sides equal

Hips level

Hips level

Knee caps face straight ahead

Knee caps face straight ahead

Feet pointing straight

Feet pointing straight

Weight equally distributed on both feet

Weight equally distributed on both feet

17

Correct Posture
(Side View)

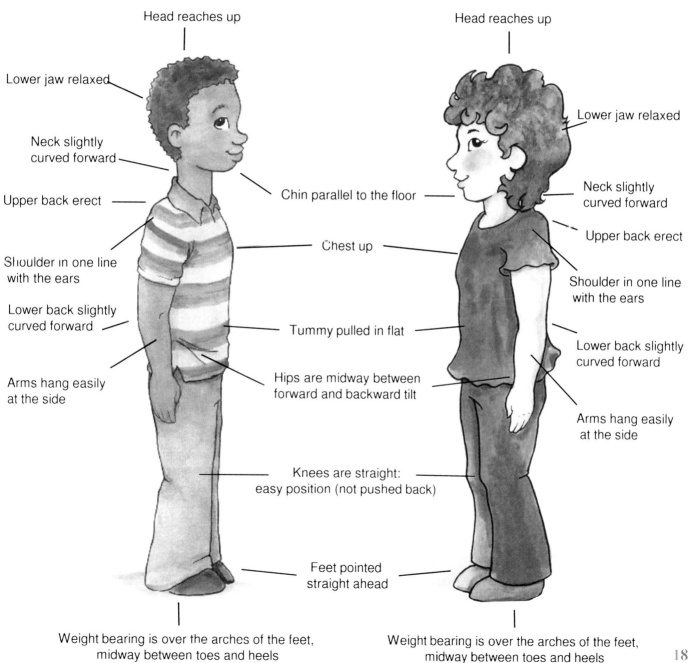

Head reaches up

Lower jaw relaxed

Neck slightly curved forward

Upper back erect

Shoulder in one line with the ears

Lower back slightly curved forward

Arms hang easily at the side

Chin parallel to the floor

Chest up

Tummy pulled in flat

Hips are midway between forward and backward tilt

Knees are straight: easy position (not pushed back)

Feet pointed straight ahead

Head reaches up

Lower jaw relaxed

Neck slightly curved forward

Upper back erect

Shoulder in one line with the ears

Lower back slightly curved forward

Arms hang easily at the side

Weight bearing is over the arches of the feet, midway between toes and heels

Weight bearing is over the arches of the feet, midway between toes and heels

18

1. <u>Arm and Leg Lift</u>
(Back Muscles)

A. Starting Position: Lie flat on the floor, face down with your arms extended beside your head.

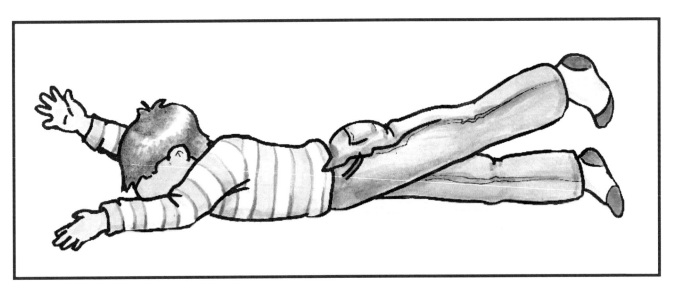

B. Lift your head off the floor and raise your right arm and your left leg. Keep the arm, leg and head 2-5 inches from the floor. Hold this position for a count of five. Alternate.

2. <u>Straight Curl Up</u>
(Abdominal Muscles)

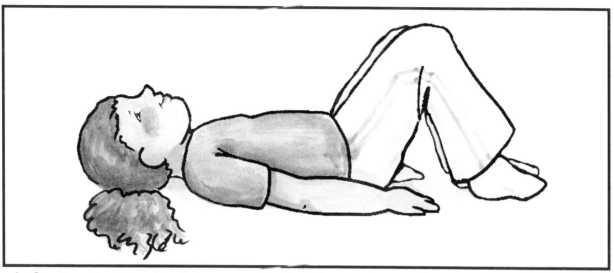

A. Starting Position: Lie flat on your back with your knees slightly bent and your arms by your side.

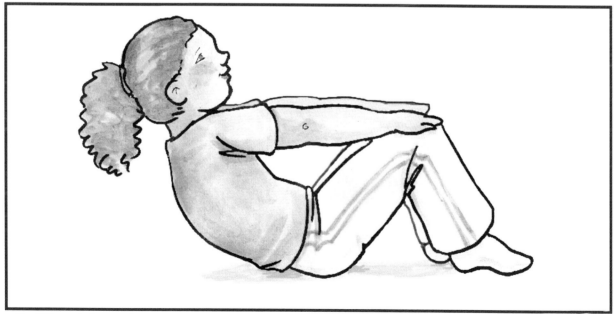

B. Tilt pelvis to flatten your back. Raise shoulders and head from the floor until your hands touch your knees. Hold this position for a count of five.

3. <u>Arch and Curve Your Back</u>

A. Starting position: Stand on hands and knees with 90 degrees between arms, body and legs.

B. Arch your back up.

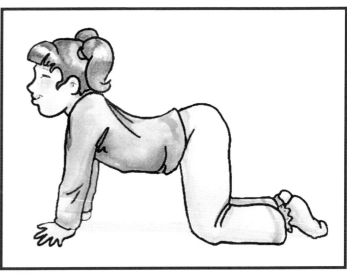

C. Curve your back down.

Keep your hands in the same position, let your back lead and the head will follow.
It is a slow movement, no need to hold position.

4. Arch and Curve Your Back with Arm and Leg Lift

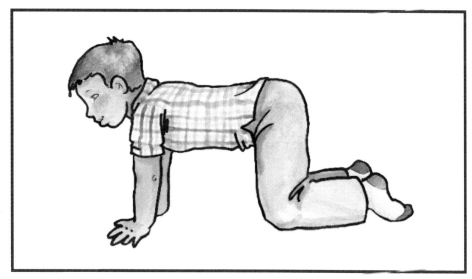

A. Starting position: Stand on your hands and knees with 90 degrees between arms, body and legs.

B. Arch your back up. Bend the right elbow backward to meet the left knee.

C. Curve your back down. Lift the right arm and the left leg up.

Alternate the movement lifting the opposite arm and leg.
It is a slow movement, no need to hold position.

5. <u>Pectoral Stretch</u>

A. Starting position: Sit up straight.

B1. Hold arms straight out, level with shoulders. Stretch arms backwards. Hold this position for a count of 5. Return to starting position.

This stretch will allow you to expand your chest and breathe better.

6. <u>Trunk Rotation</u>

7. <u>Side Bend</u>

B2. Clasp hand and extend arms in front of your body. Keep arms at shoulder level and rotate your trunk, head and arms to the left.

B3. Clasp hands over your head with arms extended. Bend to one side.

Alternate movements to the other side. Can be repeated 3- 5 times.
These are slow movements, no need to hold position.

24

8. Forward Bend

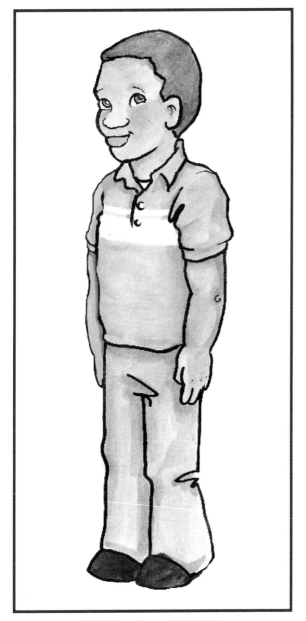

A. Stand up straight.

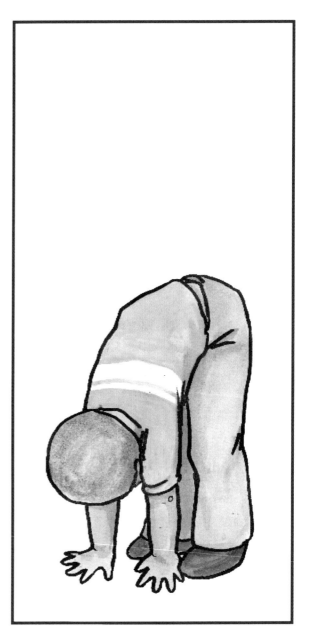

B. Bend forward.

These are slow movements, no need to hold position.

9. <u>Back and Arm Bend</u>   10. <u>Back Bend</u>

A. Starting Position: Stand up straight with your feet slightly apart.

B1. Clasp hands over your head with arms touching your ears and bend backward. Return to starting position.

B2. Place hands in the small of your back with fingers pointing downwards. Bend back.

Keep your knees straight and your head follows the trunk.
These are slow movements, no need to hold position.

Yaffa Liebermann, Physical Therapist
Geriatric Clinical Specialist
Board Certified by American Physical Therapy Association

Yaffa Liebermann was born and raised in Israel. She graduated with a degree in Physical Therapy in 1966 and moved to the United States with her husband and four children in 1986. With more than forty years of experience, Yaffa has worked in a variety of settings ranging from an acute hospital setting to in-home care.

In 1996, Yaffa founded Prime Rehabilitation Services, Inc. which is a company that provides physical, occupational and speech therapy to adults in a sub-acute setting. Yaffa is the Geriatric Liaison for the American Physical Therapy Association (APTA) of New Jersey. She serves on the Education and Best Practice Committees of The Health Care Association of New Jersey (HCANJ) for Implementing Best Practice Guideline for "Falls and Pain Management."

Yaffa is a certified Neuro-Developmental Therapist (NDT) in adult hemiplegia. She wrote a book: "Stroke Restoration- Functional Movements for Patients and Caregivers" with the illustrator Katie Sokolowski. She lectures to therapists, caregivers and communities on topics like correct breathing, exercises for wellness, proper body mechanics, and stroke restoration, amongst others.

During years of working with adults and constantly reminding them to stand up straight, Yaffa began presenting the basics of correct posture to children in schools. She has been dreaming of writing a children's book on posture for twenty years and is grateful to co-author Livia Beasley, and illustrator Katie Sokolowski, for helping her materialize her dream.

Livia Beasley, Poem Co-writer

Livia Beasley is a writer, producer and developer in children's media with 10 years of experience working in children's and family media. Livia has written television or interactive scripts for PBS, PBS Kids Sprout, Noggin, Sesame Workshop, The Learning Channel, Fisher Price, BabyFirst TV, Hooked on Phonics, Scoyo, Sockeye Media, and Wonderful Kids. Livia is also the founder of Women in Children's Media.

With heart for educating children through fun experiences, Livia chose to work with Yaffa Lieberman on "I Stand Up Straight" to help give kids a playful and musical way to remember how to keep a healthy posture.

www.liviabeasley.com

www.womeninchildrensmedia.org

Katie Sokolowski, Illustrator

Art lessons with Rachel Brooks

Katie has a Ph.D. from Rutgers Toxicology program in developmental neurotoxicology. Her interests were always rooted in natural form and were often manifested as the subjects for her paintings.

Katie worked with Yaffa Liebermann on many projects focusing on ergonomics and physical rehabilitation. "I Stand Up Straight", was a real pleasure for Katie to work on. She used bright colors to match the cheerful lyrics in order to bring correct posture into children's daily lives.

CPSIA information can be obtained
at www.ICGtesting.com
Printed in the USA
BVXC01n1702060414
349723BV00002B/4